SPEED MACHINES

LAMBORGHINI

Julia J. Quinlan

PowerKiDS press
New York

Published in 2013 by The Rosen Publishing Group, Inc.
29 East 21st Street, New York, NY 10010

First Edition

Editor: Jennifer Way
Book Design: Greg Tucker

Photo Credits: Cover, p. 19 Maksim Toome/Shutterstock.com; p. 4 © www.iStockphoto.com/Sjoerd van der Wal; pp. 5 (bottom), 9, 17, 21 KENCKOphotography/Shutterstock.com; p. 5 (top) NorGal/Shutterstock.com; p. 6 © FLPA/Richard Becker/age fotostock; pp. 7, 23, 24, 25, 26 Car Culture/Getty Images; p. 8 © Rossen Gargolov/cultu/age fotostock; p. 10 Sam Moores/Shutterstock.com; p. 11 Fedor Selivanov/Shutterstock.com; pp. 12–13 Chen Wei Seng/Shutterstock.com; p. 14 sebobeldijk/Shutterstock.com; p. 15 David Acosta Allely/Shutterstock.com; p. 16 Dongliu/Shutterstock.com; p. 18 minik/Shutterstock.com; p. 20 (main) testing/Shutterstock.com; p. 20 (inset) © eVox/age fotostock; p. 22 © www.iStockphoto.com/Lee Pettet; p. 27 dutourdumonde/Shutterstock.com; pp. 28–29 Olga Besnard/Shutterstock.com.

Library of Congress Cataloging-in-Publication Data

Quinlan, Julia J.
Lamborghini / by Julia J. Quinlan. — 1st ed.
p. cm. — (Speed machines)
Includes index.
ISBN 978-1-4488-7458-3 (library binding) — ISBN 978-1-4488-7530-6 (pbk.) —
ISBN 978-1-4488-7605-1 (6-pack)
1. Lamborghini automobile—Juvenile literature. I. Title.
TL215.L33.Q56 2013
629.222–dc23

2012003727

Manufactured in the United States of America

CPSIA Compliance Information: Batch #B4S12PK: For Further Information contact Rosen Publishing, New York, New York at 1-800-237-9932

Contents

The Charging Bull

The logo for Lamborghini is a golden charging bull. The bull represents the **astrological** sign of Taurus. This was the astrological sign of the company's founder, Ferruccio Lamborghini. The bull also is a symbol of the power under the hood of Lamborghinis. Most Lamborghinis have 12-**cylinder** engines that roar as the drivers **accelerate**. The more cylinders an engine has, the more powerful it is. The design and speed of Lamborghinis was inspired by racecars. Lamborghinis are low to the ground, accelerate quickly, and can easily make sharp turns.

The Murciélago, shown here, was one of Lamborghini's best-selling cars.

Above: Here is a Bicolore edition of the Gallardo. It is a special edition that has a two-tone paint job. *Below*: This is the Aventador, Lamborghini's latest model.

Their powerful engines and **innovative** technology keep Lamborghinis on the cutting edge of supercars. A Lamborghini's design is instantly recognizable and that is on purpose. The cars look futuristic, sleek, and stylish. One of the most popular and recognizable Lamborghini models is the Murciélago. It was made from 2001 until 2010 and more than 4,000 were sold.

From Tractors to Supercars

Most people know about the amazing supercars made by Lamborghini. Did you know that Lamborghini started out making tractors? Ferruccio Lamborghini began making tractors after World War II. By the 1950s, he began making air conditioners and gas heaters. He was so successful that he was able to live out his childhood dream and begin making cars. Lamborghini owned many luxury cars. He especially liked Ferraris, but he thought he could make an even better car!

It may seem odd to think of Lamborghini as a maker of farm equipment, but it is true! This is a Lamborghini tractor.

This is the 350 GT, Lamborghini's first production model.

In 1963, Automobili Lamborghini was founded. Its first car was introduced the same year. It was called the Lamborghini 350 GT. It was a **coupe** with two seats and a V12 engine. The V in "V12 engine" is for the shape of the engine. The number after the *V* is for how many cylinders the engine has.

By the 1970s, Ferruccio Lamborghini decided to retire and sell his company. It is currently owned by Volkswagen.

Innovative Lamborghini

The style of Lamborghinis has changed over time. The first Lamborghinis looked more like traditional sports cars, such as Ferraris. However, over time the design of Lamborghinis changed a great deal. Beginning in the 1970s, Lamborghini began making cars in its signature wedge shape. Wedge-shaped cars have a wide but short front. They get taller in the back. In the 1970s, Lamborghini also made its first car with scissor doors. Scissor doors lift up when opened.

You can see the wedge-shaped body for which Lamborghinis are known in this Gallardo.

This Lamborghini Murciélago LP640 Roadster has scissor doors.

These designs were very new and exciting in the 1970s. Lamborghini has continued to update its cars while keeping pieces of these classic designs.

Besides its innovative style, Lamborghini is known for the **engineering** and power of its cars. Lamborghini engines are so powerful that the company was hired to make engines for Formula One racecars and other kinds of racing cars.

Speedy Sports Cars

Lamborghini calls its cars super sports cars. Its super sports cars are over-the-top in many ways. They are very fast. They have an easily identifiable look. They have a futuristic design that makes them look kind of like spaceships. Lamborghini has made many different models of cars since the company's start. Even though they are all different, they are all clearly Lamborghinis. All of the current models have top speeds of at least 190 miles per hour (306 km/h) and most have top speeds of over 200 miles per hour (322 km/h).

This is a Gallardo LP 570 Spyder Performante. Having "Spyder" in a sports car's name indicates that it is a convertible.

Here is a 2012 Aventador at a motor show in Geneva, Switzerland.

In 2012, Lamborghini produced seven different car models. There is the Aventador, and there are six different types of Gallardos. It also made four special and limited-edition models. The limited-edition models are the Sesto Elemento, LP550-2 Tricolore, 560-4 Bicolore, 550-2 Bicolore, LP570-4 Super Trofeo Stradale. "Limited edition" means that Lamborghini will make only a small number of these models.

Engine Experts

Lamborghini made engines for Formula One teams from 1987 until 1993. Formula One is a type of car racing that takes place on a mix of public roads and racetracks. In 1990, Lamborghini made engines for two Formula One teams, Larousse and Lotus. The Lamborghini engines helped the Larousse team finish sixth in the World Championship in 1990. Even though Larousse had a successful season, Lamborghini did not have much more luck building engines and stopped making them for Formula One teams in 1993.

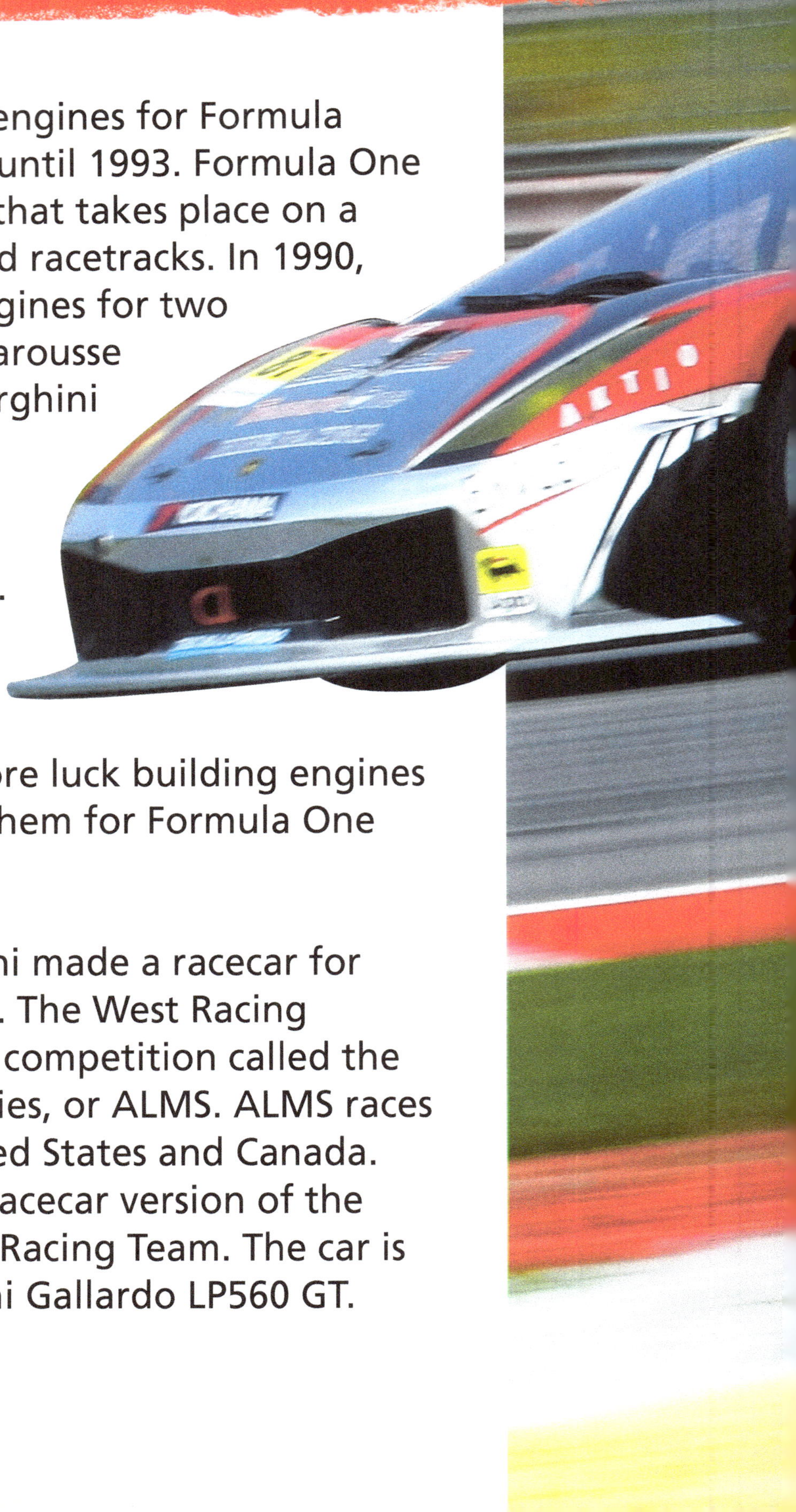

In 2011, Lamborghini made a racecar for the West Racing Team. The West Racing Team participates in a competition called the American Le Mans Series, or ALMS. ALMS races take place in the United States and Canada. Lamborghini made a racecar version of the Gallardo for the West Racing Team. The car is called the Lamborghini Gallardo LP560 GT.

The Lamborghini Gallardo GT3 was raced in the Super GT 2011 series. The car was driven by the Japanese Lamborghini Owners Club, or JLOC.

Focused on Sports Cars

Many sports car companies have racing teams. One of the most popular types of races for European companies is Formula One racing. Formula One races are called Grands Prix and take place all over the world. Formula One races feature the fastest racecars in the world. They can go up to 220 miles per hour (354 km/h). The Lamborghini Aventador can go almost as fast as Formula One cars. It has a top speed of 217 miles per hour (349 km/h).

This Gallardo is in a 2011 GT3 race in the Netherlands.

Formula One racecars have a different design from GT racecars. This is a Scuderia Ferrari Formula One car.

Lamborghini's biggest competitor, Ferrari, has a very successful Formula One team called Scuderia Ferrari. Even though Lamborghini makes very fast cars, it does not currently have a Formula One team. Lamborghini focuses on making the best super sports cars it can. It does not want to take its focus away from that.

Aventador

The Aventador replaced the very popular Murciélago. It was introduced in 2010. Lamborghini started from scratch and redesigned every part of the car. The Aventador is still clearly a Lamborghini. It looks like something from the future. The Aventador has scissor doors, which Lamborghini is known for. The doors do not open out to the side, as most car doors do. They open straight up. This makes it very eye-catching, but it also makes the car impractical for normal parking situations.

Here you can see the scissor doors that the Aventador is known for. Its lightweight, carbon-fiber body helps make it a super fast car.

Lamborghini Aventador

Engine size	6.5 liters
Number of cylinders	12
Transmission	Manual (stick shift)
Gearbox	7 speeds
0–60 mph (0–97 km/h)	2.9 seconds
Top speed	217 mph (349 km/h)

The Aventador's body sits very low to the ground. That is why the car needs hydraulic lifts to keep from ruining the body on bumpy roads!

Like all Lamborghinis, the Aventador is fast. Its top speed is 217 miles per hour (349 km/h). It has a V12 engine and 691 **horsepower**. It accelerates extremely quickly. It can reach 60 miles per hour (97 km/h) in just 2.9 seconds. It has all-wheel drive. The Aventador is so low to the ground that it has special **hydraulic** lifts that bring the car up 1.6 inches (4 cm) so drivers can get over bumps safely.

Gallardo

Gallardo is a series of cars produced by Lamborghini. The Gallardos are named after a famous fighting bull. There have been several different models made since the Gallardo's beginning in 2003. In 2012, Lamborghini made six different kinds of Gallardos. They are the LP570-4 Superleggera, LP560-4, LP550-2, LP570-4 Spyder Performante, LP560-4 Spyder, and the LP550-2 Spyder. The Gallardos are the first Lamborghinis to have iPod connections and USB ports.

The Gallardo is Lamborghini's most produced car model.

LP570-4 Superleggera

Engine size	5.2 liters
Number of cylinders	10
Transmission	Manual
Gearbox	6 speeds
0–62 mph (0–100 km/h)	3.4 seconds
Top speed	202 mph (325 km/h)

The first version of the Lamborghini Gallardo Superleggera, shown here, came out in 2007.

The LP570-4 Superleggera was introduced in 2010. It was made to be lighter than previous models. *Superleggera* means "super light" in Italian. Making the car lighter makes it able to go faster. The Superleggera has a top speed of 202 miles per hour (325 km/h). It can go from 0 to 60 miles per hour (0–97 km/h) in 3.4 seconds and can get up to 124 miles per hour (200 km/h) in only 10.2 seconds!

Murciélago

The Murciélago was one of Lamborghini's most popular models. It was made from 2001 until 2010, and 4,099 cars were sold. The Murciélago replaced the Diablo. The first Murciélago model was called simply the Lamborghini Murciélago. Later models had different names so people could tell them apart.

Top: Here is the engine of a 2008 Murciélago LP640. *Bottom*: The Murciélago LP670-4 SuperVeloce has scissor doors. Unlike regular car doors, scissor doors connect to the body the same way on both hardtops and convertibles.

Murciélago LP670-4 SuperVeloce

Engine size	6.5 liters
Number of cylinders	12
Transmission	Manual
Gearbox	6 speeds
0–62 mph (0–100 km/h)	3.2 seconds
Top speed	212 mph (341 km/h)

Here is a Murciélago LP670-4 SuperVeloce. *Super veloce* is Italian for "super fast"!

The 2001 model can reach 60 miles per hour (97 km/h) in 3.6 seconds. It can get to 116 miles per hour (187 km/h) in 11.6 seconds. It has a V12 engine and a 6-gear manual **transmission**. The Murciélago has a top speed of 205 miles per hour (330 km/h). The last Murciélago model was introduced in 2009. It is called the Murciélago LP670-4 SuperVeloce. The SuperVeloce is faster than the original Murciélago. It can go from 0 to 62 miles per hour (0–100 km/h) in 3.2 seconds and has a top speed of 212 miles per hour (341 km/h).

Diablo

The Lamborghini Diablo was first introduced in 1990. At the time, it was the fastest **production** car ever made. The Diablo's top speed was 202 miles per hour (325 km/h). It was a two-seater with 458 horsepower and a V12 engine. The Diablo had a manual 5-speed transmission. It could go from 0 to 60 miles per hour (0–97 km/h) in 3.9 seconds and get to 80 miles per hour (129 km/h) in 9.6 seconds. The Diablo had Lamborghini's signature scissor doors.

The Diablo was the first Lamborghini to have a top speed of over 200 miles per hour (322 km/h).

Diablo VT 6.0

Engine size	6.0 liters
Number of cylinders	12
Transmission	Manual
Gearbox	5 speeds
0–60 mph (0–97 km/h)	3.4 seconds
Top speed	202 mph (325 km/h)

This 2000 Diablo GT has a bright and flashy interior design.

The 2001 Diablo VT 6.0 and VT 6.0 SE were the last Diablos produced. The last model of the Diablo has much in common with the first, including a five-speed manual transmission and a V12 engine. The VT 6.0 is more powerful, though. It has 550 horsepower and can reach 60 miles per hour (97 km/h) in 3.4 seconds.

350 GT

The 350 GT was the first car built by Lamborghini. GTs, or grand tourers, are luxury cars that are made to be driven long distances. There were 120 of these cars made from 1963 until 1966. Ferruccio Lamborghini made the 350 GT to compete with Ferraris. He wanted his new car to be faster, better looking, and more powerful than any of Ferrari's cars. Ferruccio Lamborghini believed that the 350 GT could compete with the Ferrari 250.

The Ferrari 250, shown here, was the car that inspired Lamborghini to create the 350 GT.

Lamborghini 350 GT

Engine size	3.5 liters
Number of cylinders	12
Transmission	Manual
Gearbox	5 speeds
0–60 mph (0–97 km/h)	6.8 seconds
Top speed	160 mph (257 km/h)

The Lamborghini 350 GT, shown here, was produced from 1964 until 1966.

The 350 GT had 280 horsepower and could go up to 160 miles per hour (257 km/h). It could reach 62 miles per hour (100 km/h) in 6.8 seconds and reach 100 miles per hour (161 km/h) in 16.3 seconds. The 350 GT was a coupe. A coupe is a two-door car. Most coupes can have two or three seats.

Countach

The Lamborghini Countach started what is now known as Lamborghini's signature style. It was the first Lamborghini to have scissor doors. It was also the first to have the wedge shape that many Lamborghinis have. The Countach was a two-seater that was very low to the ground. The Countach's engine was in the back of the car, rather than in the front. Because of this, the driver and passenger seats were pushed forward. The Countach was made from 1974 until 1990, and 2,000 of the cars were sold. Lamborghini made eight different models of the Countach, each more powerful than the last.

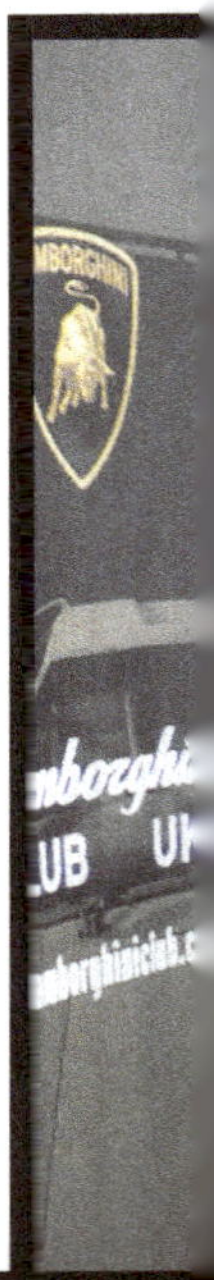

In the Countach, you can see the beginning of the classic Lamborghini low-sitting, wedge-shaped body.

Countach

Engine size	4.0 liters
Number of cylinders	12
Transmission	Manual
Gearbox	5 speeds
0–60 mph (0–97 km/h)	5.1 seconds
Top speed	186 mph (299 km/h)

The 25th Anniversary Countach, shown here, was named to honor Lamborghini's twenty-fifth year of producing cars.

The first version of the Countach was the Countach LP400. It was made from 1974 until 1976. It had a 4.0-liter V12 engine. It had 370 horsepower and could go from 0 to 60 miles per hour (0–97 km/h) in 5.1 seconds.

Charging into the Future

Lamborghini continues to produce some of the most eye-catching and innovative super sports cars in the world. Besides its current models in production, Lamborghini makes concept cars. Concept cars will not necessarily go into production. They are innovative ideas for cars. In 2008, Lamborghini showed a concept car called the Estoque. The Estoque would have been the first four-door sedan made by Lamborghini. For now, the Estoque is still just an idea.

In 2010, Lamborghini showed the Sesto Elemento, which is Italian for "sixth **element**." The car is made out of carbon fiber. Carbon fiber is extremely light. The Sesto Elemento is not as fast as other Lamborghinis, with a top speed of over 185 miles per hour (298 km/h). However, it can accelerate very fast because it is so light.

Lamborghini has always worked to improve its cars. It continues to make its cars faster, more powerful, and more eye-catching.

The Sesto Elemento is the lightest car Lamborghini has ever produced. It weighs only 2,200 pounds (998 kg).

Comparison Chart

CAR	YEARS MADE	SALES	TOP SPEED	FACT
Aventador	2010–	4,000	217 mph (349 km/h)	Named after a bull from Saragossa, Spain.
Gallardo	2003–	10,000	202 mph (325 km/h)	*Gallardo* means "brave and graceful" in Spanish.
Murciélago	2001–2010	4,099	212 mph (341 km/h)	The name means "bat" in Spanish. It was also the name of a famous Spanish fighting bull.
Diablo	1990–2001	2,884	202 mph (325 km/h)	Its name means "devil" in Spanish.
350 GT	1964–1966	120	160 mph (257 km/h)	Debuted at the 1964 Geneva Auto Show.
Countach	1974–1990	2,042	186 mph (299 km/h)	*Countach* is an Italian exclamation meaning "oh wow!" or "holy smokes!"

Glossary

accelerate (ik-SEH-luh-rayt) To increase in speed.

astrological (as-truh-LO-jih-kul) Having to do with the effect some believe the stars and planets have on people's lives.

cylinder (SIH-len-der) The enclosed space for a piston in an engine.

coupe (KOOP) A kind of car with two doors and a hard roof.

element (EH-luh-ment) The basic matter of which all things are made.

engineering (en-juh-NEER-ing) Making and using technology.

horsepower (HORS-pow-er) The way an engine's power is measured. One horsepower is the power to lift 550 pounds (250 kg) 1 foot (.3 m) in 1 second.

hydraulic (hy-DRO-lik) A system of tubes that lift and lower the body of a car when oil is pushed through them.

innovative (IH-nuh-vay-tiv) Making something new.

production (pruh-DUK-shun) Made to sell.

transmission (trans-MIH-shun) A group of parts that includes the gears for changing speeds and that conveys the power from the engine to the machine's rear wheel.

Index

Websites

Due to the changing nature of Internet links, PowerKids Press has developed an online list of websites related to the subject of this book. This site is updated regularly. Please use this link to access the list:
www.powerkidslinks.com/smach/lambo/